JELLY BEANS

by Dennis Miller

Illustrated by Mary Lynn Baird

JELLY BEANS
Copyright © 2002 by Dennis Miller

Illustrations by Mary Lynn Baird

Published in Loveland, Colorado, by Twin Peaks Publishing, Inc.
Printed by: Boomer's Printing Company
Bound by: Pease Bindery, Inc.
               Lincoln, Nebraska
               United States of America

Library of Congress Cataloging-in-Publication Data
Miller, Dennis
    Jelly Beans / Dennis Miller; illustrated by Mary Lynn Baird.
    Summary: Jelly beans come alive and talk to humans about diversity, character,
        and how they get along with each other despite their different colors.
            1. Children's stories, American. [1. Jelly beans - Fiction]
            I. Baird, Mary Lynn, ill.   II. Title

ISBN 0-9722259-0-0

Thanks to Mom for love and reading when I was three.

Thanks to Mrs. Arnessen who believed in the writer I could be.

Thanks to Mary Lynn and Amber who made beans come alive.

Thanks to Barbara who gently encouraged me to strive.

And, thanks to you, too!

Dennis

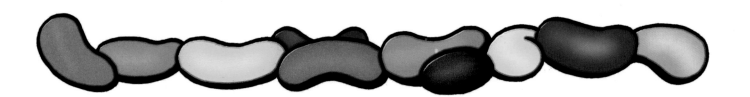

I bought a bag of jelly beans

A day or so ago,

And never really paid them mind

For how was I to know...

That they would have a tale to tell

About the facts of life,

And how the people of our world

Could save themselves some strife.

But when I opened up that bag

And watched the beans spill out,

They huddled close together there

And they began to shout!

They stood on end and waddled

On my kitchen table top,

In throngs of many colors bright

Their voices would not stop!

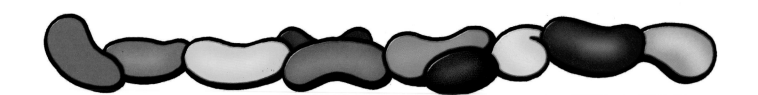

"Now we all have some things to say

About you human folks,

And now that we are out and free

You'll have to take our pokes."

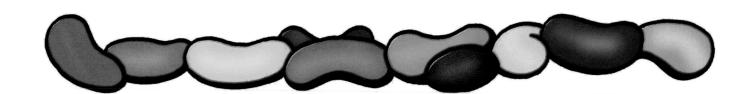

"As you can see, we all have shapes

And our sizes aren't the same,

The factory mixed us up like this

So we are not to blame."

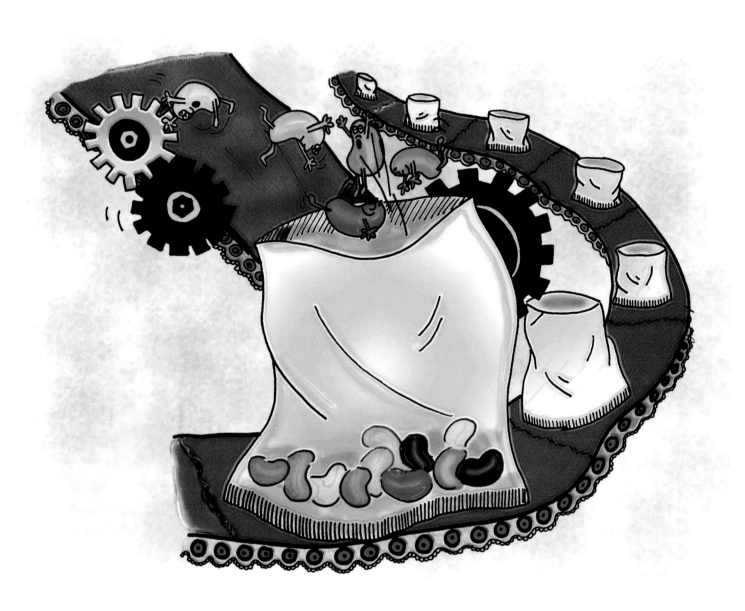

"But we are special <u>human beans</u>

We live together well,

Not one of us is without fault

But each of us is swell!"

"For we discovered very soon

Each bean is made unique,

And color, shape, and flavors, too

Can differ, yet be sweet."

"So now that you have let us out

We wanted you to know,

That human <u>beings</u> are just like us

But you won't let it show."

"Instead of judging by the heart

You judge by different skins,

And those of you with different shapes

Must suffer others' whims."

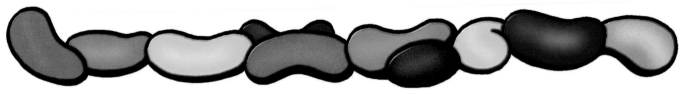

"We want to tell you that your world

Could be like that of ours,

If you decide to look inside

Behind the years of scars."

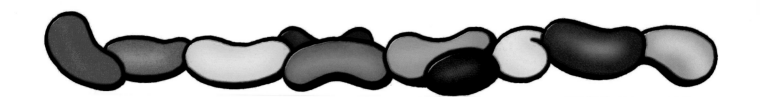

"If candy beans can do it

In our bagged world very small,

We're very sure there's hope for you

Up there where all is tall."

"So now that we have had our say

We're set to treat your taste,

Go ahead and gobble all of us

For candy's not to waste."

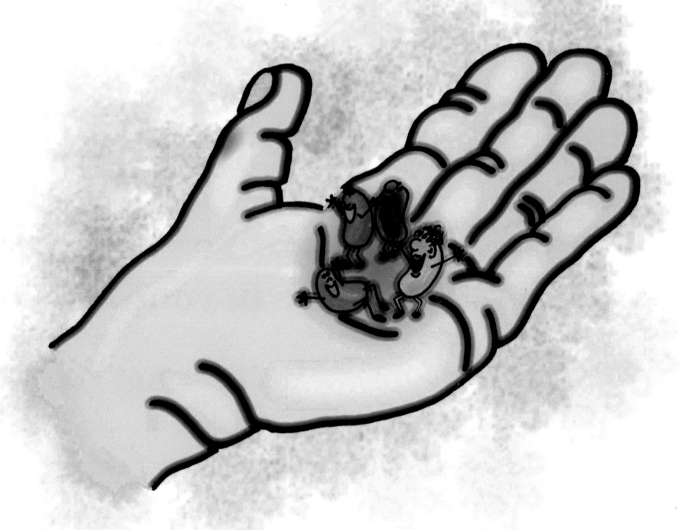

"But think about the things we've said

And even when we're gone,

Our message will be in your head

To guide you all life long."

I don't believe I've lost my mind

I don't reside in dreams,

But never have I had a chat

With lowly jelly beans!

But I can tell you this for sure

For there is little doubt,

I'll never eat another one

Until I've checked it out!

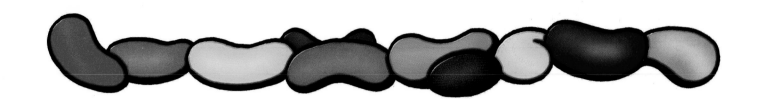

That magic bag of human beans

Sure changed my point of view,

And made me think about our world...

Will you be thinking, too?

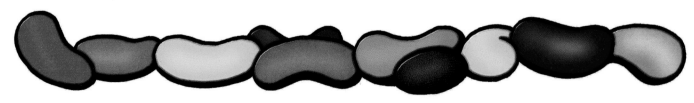

About the Author...

Dennis Miller left public education after twenty-five years to pursue a lifelong goal of writing. His books talk about diversity and character in a new colorful way. Dennis lives with his wife, Barbara, and their miniature schnauzer, Molly, in Loveland, Colorado. His three sons, Mark, Erik, and James, live nearby so there are opportunities for Rockies baseball games and golfing. Drop in anytime, there's always a full jar of jelly beans on his desk!

About the Illustrator...

Mary Lynn Baird has been a mentor to budding elementary school artists for fifteen years; she now teaches art in Englewood, Colorado. In 1999, she was named "Colorado Elementary Art Educator of the Year". Her husband Mike and three children (Hannah, Madison, and Landon) live in Littleton where Mary Lynn is co-owner of a furniture painting business called "2 Wacky Chics". Her other work includes *A Children's Ministry*, a book by Group Publishing. Mary Lynn's artistic creativity is a key element of the magic that brings *Jelly Beans* to life.

Twin Peaks Publishing, Inc.
<u>Order Form</u>

**Want more *Jelly Beans*? Just complete the
following five steps and mail your order to us.**

1. Name _____

 Address _____

 City _____ State _____ Zip _____

2. Qty _____ @ $15.95   = $ _____

 Tax* @ 3.8%   = $ _____

 Shipping/Handling (see below**)   = $ _____

 Total Order $ _____

 * Colorado residents only
 ** One book $3.50
   For each additional book, add $2.00

3. Please enclose your check or money order made to:
 Twin Peaks Publishing, Inc.

4. If you wish to have your book(s) autographed by the author, please
indicate to whom it should be addressed:

 Book #1: _____ Book # 7: _____
 Book #2: _____ Book# 8: _____
 Book #3: _____ Book# 9: _____
 Book #4: _____ Book# 10: _____
 Book #5: _____ Book# 11: _____
 Book #6: _____ Book# 12: _____

5. Please Mail This Form to: **Twin Peaks Publishing, Inc.**
                      4708 Mountain Vista Court
                      Loveland, CO 80537

What others are saying about *Jelly Beans...*

"Through the imaginary world of *Jelly Beans*, Mr. Miller has cleverly engaged students in the path of personal self-reflection and the discovery of their values. Children are taken into a make-believe world where "Human Beans" are all similar, yet look very different. This is so like the world around us today, and enables this book to have tremendous staying power. Through the lively art of rollicking rhymes, Mr. Miller has magically blended together the essence of diversity in a story format especially enjoyed by elementary aged students."

> Gail Holben
> Elementary School Principal
> Fort Collins, Colorado

"I used this book in my first grade class and the kids were called the jelly beans. The book's vocabulary is higher level, but it is used in such appropriate context that first graders are still able to understand the message! The message of *Jelly Beans* is critical for all ages of students!"

> Allison Thomas
> Elementary School Teacher
> Corning, Iowa

"*Jelly Beans* celebrates our collective diversities and challenges us to work towards a better world. Dennis Miller has presented in a profound and entertaining manner this complicated and highly emotional concept in terms the very young can grasp. Children will be clamoring to hear this again and again."

> Julie Wilcox
> Elementary School Librarian
> Loveland, Colorado

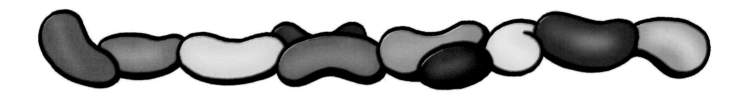